One Fat Cat

WRITTEN BY
VIVIAN FRENCH

ILLUSTRATED BY
LIZ MILLION

WALKER BOOKS
AND SUBSIDIARIES
LONDON • BOSTON • SYDNEY

For Philip, with love
L.M.

First published 2001 by Walker Books Ltd
87 Vauxhall Walk, London SE11 5HJ

2 4 6 8 10 9 7 5 3 1

Text © 2001 Vivian French
Illustrations © 2001 Liz Million

This book has been typeset in Century Old Style

Printed in Hong Kong

British Library Cataloguing in Publication Data:
a catalogue record for this book is
available from the British Library

ISBN 0-7445-8311-X

Notes for Children

This book is a little different from other picture books.
You will be sharing it with other people and telling
the story together.

You can read

this line

this line

or this line.

Even when someone else is reading, try to follow
the words. It will help when it's your turn!

One fat cat

Sleeping.

Purr purr!

Purr purr purr!

Cat on a mat

Sleeping.

Two little mice

Peeping.

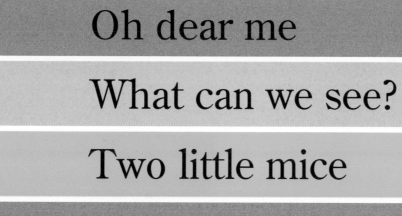

Oh dear me

What can we see?

Two little mice

Peeping.

One fat cat

Waking.

Meow meow!

Dinner time now!

One fat cat

Waking.

Two little mice

Shaking.

Eek eek eek!

Squeak squeak squeak!

Two little mice

Shaking.

One fat cat

Drinking.

Sip sip sip!

Lap lap lap!

One fat cat

Drinking.

Two little mice

Thinking.

We see a cat

We don't like that!

Two little mice

Thinking.

One fat cat

Sniffing.

Is there a mouse

A mouse in the house?

One fat cat

Sniffing.

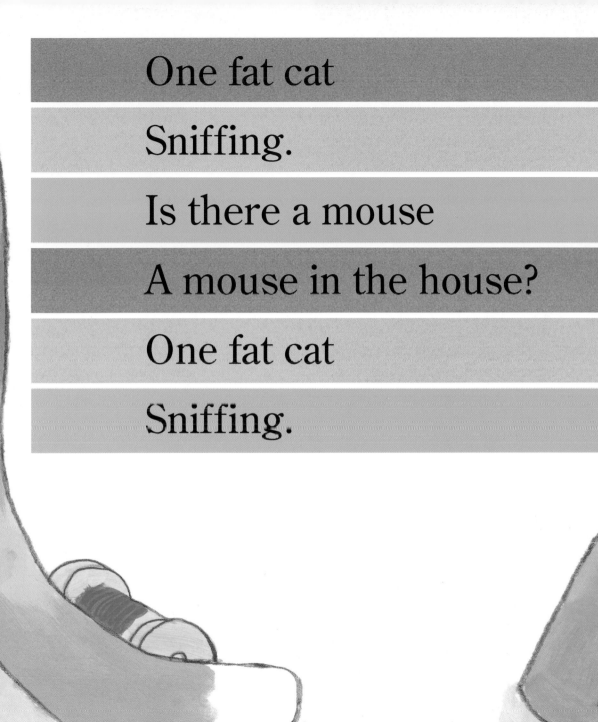

Two little mice

Puffing.

Push push push!

Push push push!

Two little mice

Puffing.

One fat cat

Hunting.

Hunting here!

Hunting there!

One fat cat

Hunting.

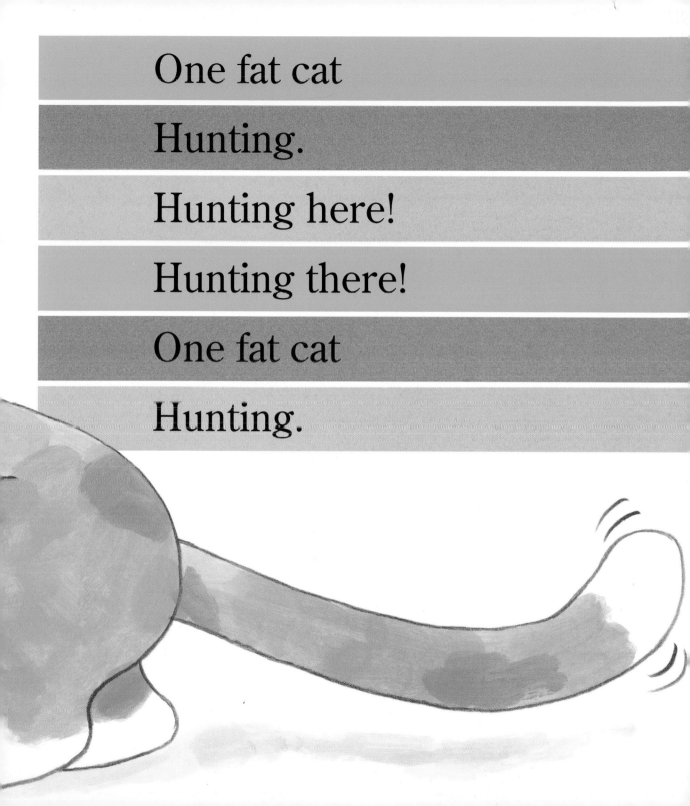

Two little mice

Grunting.

Ready

Steady

One two three

PUSH!

CRASH!

One fat cat

Leaping.

Meow meow!

Run away now!

One fat cat

Leaping.

Two little mice

Sleeping.

Snore snore

Snore some more.

Two little mice

Sleeping.

Notes for Teachers

Story Plays are written and presented in a way that encourages children to read aloud together. They are exciting stories, told in strongly patterned language which gives children the chance to practise at a vital stage of their reading development. Sharing stories in this way makes reading an active and enjoyable process, and one that draws in even the reticent reader.

The story is told by three different voices, divided into three colours so that each child can easily read his or her part. When there are more than three children in a group, there is an ideal opportunity for paired reading. Partnering a more experienced reader with a less experienced one can be very supportive and provides a learning experience for both children.

Story Plays encourage children to share in the reading of a whole text in a collaborative and interactive way. This makes them perfect for group and guided reading activities. Children will find they need to pay close attention to the print and punctuation, and to use the meaning of the whole story in order to read it with expression and a real sense of voice.